Speedy the Turtle

Story by Jessica Sterling-Malek
Illustrations by Jason Goad

Copyright 2014

**Dedicated to Sasha and JD
and to
Belvedere Nursery School**

"Mommy! I had so much fun at school today!"

"Oh, good," said Mommy.

"What did you do?

Who did you play with?"

"I played with Olivia,
Sidney, Audrey, Somerset,
and Speedy!"

"Speedy?" Mommy asked.
"Speedy who?"

"Speedy the turtle, Silly!
Did you forget who Speedy is?"

"Today my teacher, Mrs. Parker, took Speedy out of his tank at circle time. Speedy and I danced together."

"When I ate my ham and cheese sandwich for lunch, Speedy ate worms!

Eww!

But he had strawberries for dessert. Yummy!"

"And Speedy played outside with me in the grass. It was soooooo fun!"

"Mommy, remember when I used to cry because I didn't want to go to school?

Then one day you gave me strawberries to feed Speedy.

That made me happy. He was my first friend at school."

"Mommy, may I bring
Speedy home for a playdate?"

"A playdate with a turtle?"
Mommy said.

"Please, Mommy! Please, Mommy!
Plllllease!"

"I'm not sure that's such
a great idea, Sasha."

"Mommy if you let me
have a playdate..."

"Oh my. I don't think Speedy can leave the school, " Mommy said. "The school is his home. He's lived there for more than thirty years!"

"Does Speedy play with the toys
and dance at night
while the kids are away from school?"

We learned that Speedy is a box turtle, and he's a boy because his eyes are red and orange.

Girl turtles have yellow or brown eyes.

Speedy sleeps at night and
also naps during the day

He doesn't sleep
with a blanket, but during
the colder months,
he needs a heating pad
and a heat lamp to stay warm.

Speedy could live to be eighty years old. That's really old!

Speedy has a hinged shell.

He can crawl inside his shell to hide when he's scared.

I learned so much about box turtles
that the next day at school,
I asked my teacher, Mrs. Parker,
if I could take Speedy home for a
playdate since I knew
I could take care of him.

She smiled and told me Speedy
needs to stay at school.

So I won't get a playdate after all,
but I'll get to play with Speedy
everyday at school.

"This is his home.

And he's happy here!"

DRAW SPEEDY!

Made in the USA
San Bernardino, CA
22 July 2014